SUPER SPLENDOUR BOOKS

II

IN THE SUPER SPLENDOUR BOOK SERIES

IN THE SPLENDOUR BOOK SERIES

IN THE JUNIOR SPLENDOUR BOOK SERIES

MADE AND PRINTED IN ITALY BY FRATELLI FABBRI EDITORI, MILAN,
FOR THE PUBLISHERS, W. H. ALLEN AND CO. LTD., ESSEX STREET, LONDON, WC2.
PUBLISHED IN AUSTRALIA BY GOLDEN PRESS PTY. LTD., SYDNEY
© FRATELLI FABBRI EDITORI, 1961

TALES From RUSSIA

RETOLD BY
SHIRLEY GOULDEN

ILLUSTRATED BY
BENVENUTI

W. H. ALLEN

Contents

TALES from RUSSIA

The Tale of
The Firebird

Once Russia was a land divided, and ruled by various Czars. Some of the Czars were weak, a few strong, one or two good, the rest bad; not so different, in fact from other folk, except for the blood in their veins—and that was supposed to be blue.

It is said that magic was the order of those days, and happened as naturally as mischief happens to you, but one can never be sure of the truth, times having changed so. Though to be sure the story of Prince Ivan and the Firebird was no ordinary affair, as you shall hear.

Ivan's father was one of the weaker Czars, but his estates were vast. Within his domain stood a palace where Ivan lived with his two brothers, Dimitri and Vassily, and in the palace garden there grew a wonderful apple tree. It was no different from any other tree as to bark and leaves and branches. The apples, however, (when in season) were solid gold to the core. Naturally the Czar valued this tree beyond everything, and was therefore most upset one day to find that two of his precious gold apples were missing. Concealed behind the topiary hedge, the Czar set himself to catch the thief. Nothing happened until after nightfall, by which time, the Czar was cold as well as hungry. Then, in a rush of wings and sudden warmth, a great bird, all aglow and resplendent arrived, lighting the garden with its brilliance, and striking golden sparks from the apples on the tree. Before the Czar dared or cared (for fear of burning his fingers) to stop it, the Firebird plucked a golden apple and flew away.

Courage not being one of his strong points but greed being one of his weaknesses (I told you he had them), the Czar thought he would stay safely at home and send his sons after the Firebird.

"It stands to reason," he told them. "If the Firebird has my golden apples, I am entitled to have the Firebird! So whoever captures or kills this creature shall be my heir."

"I am your heir in any case, being the eldest," objected Dimitri, who was lazy and did not see why he should seek a favour that was his already.

"Being second to the eldest, I am your heir, should anything befall Dimitri," put in Vassily, who cared more for himself than anyone else.

"That," said the Czar, "is for me to decide. My estates will pass not to the elder but to the better." "Best," corrected Ivan. "There *are* three of us you know, father." The Czar was inclined to overlook Ivan, since he was a good deal younger than the others. "Try if you like boy," he shrugged, "though a frail lad like you will have small chance against the Firebird. My advice is to stay out of it." This of course made Ivan more determined

than either of his brothers to succeed.

They decided to take it in turns to keep watch near the apple tree, as the Czar had done, in the belief that the Firebird would return for another apple. Dimitri, as the eldest, agreed somewhat reluctantly, to take first watch. By nightfall he felt so sleepy that the Firebird was almost upon him, in a flash of hot flame, before he saw it. Jumping to his feet in alarm Dimitri plucked a silver arrow from his quiver and aimed, as the Firebird swooped overhead to-wards the apple tree. His aim was true enough and the arrow struck the Firebird. Yet instead of injuring it, the arrow melted and bent in the heat of the bird's body, and fell harmless to the ground. He had disturbed the bird however, and it flew off, singeing Dimitri's waxed moust-ache, and so the prince had to return and admit that he had failed to bring down the Firebird.

Vassily, now seeing the kingdom within his grasp, took a large net of chain-mail and settled down behind the hedge near the apple tree, ready for the Firebird's next visit. It was not long in coming, for a golden apple melts lusciously in the mouth of a Firebird in the same way that the red-ripe kind melts in yours.

There came a clapping of wings and the smell of burning leaves. Vassily lifted his net of mail and flung it far above his head, as the air grew suddenly warm. A shower of sparks de-scended as the net closed about the Firebird, pricking Vassily's skin like a million falling needles. Still the thought of his father's king-dom made Vassily hold tightly on to the net, and he hauled downwards, thinking to have trapped the fabulous bird. The mail, however, was no proof against the flames that ate into it from the Firebird's body. The chains melted apart, and in a moment the Firebird was freed and had flown away, taking with it not only Vassily's hopes of becoming his father's heir, but another golden apple as well. Thus Vassily returned to the palace, having fared no better than his brother. The Czar was not pleased—he seldom was when his orders were disobeyed—and the two elder brothers slunk away in disgrace. Only Ivan remained to retrieve the family honour, and he made up his mind to catch the Firebird if it took the whole of his life to do so. That night he too, lay in wait behind the hedge near the precious apple tree. Far away in the night sky a point of light showed, swooping rapidly like a falling star. The light grew nearer until Ivan could see that it came from the great glowing bird. Orange and yellow flames darted from its body, making the air hot and moist, as the Firebird came onwards. Instead of remaining behind the hedge as his brothers had done, Ivan climbed nimbly up the apple tree, and when the Firebird swooped to take one of the golden apples he cooly (in spite of the intense heat) put out his hand and grabbed the bird's tail. It was terribly hot but Ivan held on grimly as the Firebird tugged frantically upwards. Something had to give, and something did—it was the Firebirds' tail. Ivan was left holding a shimmering feather, but the Firebird had escaped and was winging away into the distance. Dropping the feather from one hand to another like a hot potato, Ivan went to fetch his horse, for he meant to go on with the hunt. Though he had caught only a painful blister instead of the Firebird, the feather lit a path through the darkness, making a splendid torch. Ivan rode for three nights through the golden shaft of brilliance that shone from the feather, which he had put in his hat. During

the day when the light of the feather waned in the rays of the sun, he slept and refreshed himself with berries and clear stream water. Ivan felt that sooner or later the feather would lead him to the Firebird. On the sixth night of the journey a sleek grey wolf sudenly leaped out of a thicket and frightened Ivan's horse so that it tumbled him off, head-over-heels, and galloped away in terror. Ivan picked himself up and surveyed the wolf with natural caution. Fortunately this particular wolf had just had his supper, and appeared to be in a pleasant mood. In any case, it was no ordinary wolfish wolf, but a magic animal, who was attracted by the mystical light of the feather in Ivan's hat. "Greetings," said the wolf encouragingly. "What brings you to these parts, my young traveller?"

"I am in search of the Firebird, who has stolen some golden apples from my father's tree," said Ivan, much relieved by the wolf's evident good will. "But how can I continue now that my horse has bolted?" The wolf bared his teeth in a smile. "That I fear is my fault," he replied. "I did appear on the scene rather unexpectedly, to be sure. One of my habits, you know, is to surprise rather than be surprised. Allow me to make amends and carry you the rest of the way myself."

Ivan decided to trust the wolf, for without his help he could certainly never hope to find the Firebird, now that the horse had gone. Climbing on the wolf's back they went away with astonishing speed, along the path of light shed by the golden feather through the midnight gloom.

At daybreak when the feather torch began to dim, they came up to a great wall, and the wolf invited Ivan to stand on his back, so that he might scale it. "That is where you will find the Firebird," said the wolf. "Take care, my friend, not to get burned."—Ivan thanked the wolf for his kindness, found a firm foothold in the wall, and clambered over into the garden. It was not hard to see the Firebird, for the amazing creature was comfortably settled on a huge bonfire, in the centre lawn, before a palace of many spires. Ivan approached warily, remembering the wolf's warning, and wondered how he could capture the Firebird without putting his hand into the flaming bonfire. After some thought Ivan stooped and picking up a stone threw it at his quarry. The Firebird squawked indignantly and rose from its bed of flames. White hot with fury it encircled the garden, setting alight branches and bushes with its fiery wings. The smoke and flames attracted attention from inside the palace, and soon the guards were out, throwing pails of water about to douse the flames. In all the confusion Ivan darted after the Firebird and leaping high in the air, managed to grab one of its hot feet and bring the bird down. It beat its wings on the smouldering grass and sent up such a smoke that the guards left the rest of the garden crackling merrily and dashed to the scene. "Here is the villain who is causing all the trouble!" they cried. "He is trying to steal the Firebird!" Ivan surrounded on all sides by the enemy was soon hustled into the palace of the rich Czar Dolmat. When the Czar heard that Ivan had tried to take the wonderful Firebird, and had wrecked his garden too, he was very angry indeed, and said that Ivan should pay with his life.

10

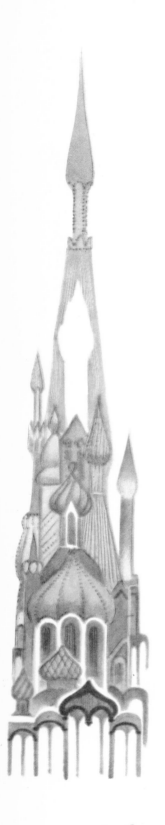

"Allow me to explain, dear sir," said Ivan, who by this time was a good deal hot and bothered. "Your bird is the thief, not I; for it has been stealing apples from the tree of my father, Czar Vyslav, in the neighbouring kingdom. It has swallowed so many apples that my father considers the bird belongs to him."

"If that is the case," said Czar Dolmat, who was a just, if hasty man, "you shall take the Firebird back to your father. But first I must have something in its place. In the kingdom of Czar Afron there is a horse with a golden mane. That would be fair exchange for the Firebird."

"I daresay it would," thought Ivan, "though what Czar Afron will have to say remains to be heard." However, it was clear now that in all honour he was obliged to make some return to Czar Dolmat for the Firebird.

When Ivan came out of the garden, through a pair of heavy gates this time, the faithful wolf was still waiting to see how he had fared. Ivan explained that he now had a new quest, in the kingdom of Czar Afron, and the wolf, ever obliging, offered to take him there.

The way was far, but the wolf ran with the wind, and they soon came to the white stables of Czar Afron. Night had fallen once again, and as Ivan crept inside the stables, none stopped him, for all the grooms were fast asleep. Among the horses, shifting their hooves and whinneying restlessly, one stood out plainly in the dark, for it was snow white with a mane of bright gold. On the wall nearby Ivan saw a golden bridle, and lifting it down he began to harness the wonderful white horse. Unfortunately, the bridle had little gold bells hanging from it, and they set up such a jingling and jangling that the grooms were instantly aroused from their slumber. Once again Ivan was made prisoner and taken before the Czar, accused of stealing his golden-maned horse.

"If there's anything I can't abide, it's a horse thief!" thundered Czar Afron, who was extremely short-tempered at the best of times—and this was by no means the best of times. Ivan flushed as hotly as if the Firebird were there. "Indeed sir, I am no thief but the son of a Czar like yourself," he protested.

"Then behave like the son of a Czar and stop sneaking into other people's stables and taking other people's horses, without any thought of replacing them!" snapped Czar Afron.

"I would willingly bring whatever you wish, in return for the golden-

maned horse," said Ivan, anxious to prove his honourable intentions.

"Then bring me the beautiful Princess Helen who lives on the Steppes, for my wife," said Czar Afron. "I myself have asked her time and again, but strangely enough she will not have me." Ivan thought this was not by any means strange, for Czar Afron was rather ugly, as well as being bad-tempered. However he agreed that Princess Helen should be exchanged for the horse, and went off to find her at once. Ivan saw that the wolf had not deserted him, but was waiting near the stables. Hastily he explained what had to be done, and the wolf carried him on his back to the snowy Steppes where Princess Helen lived in an iron stronghold.

When they arrived in that bleak and blowy place, the wolf bounded across the iron drawbridge, Ivan clinging to his neck, across the courtyard of the castle, and in at an open bedroom window. There lay Princess Helen, half asleep, and if the speed of their arrival had not already taken Ivan's breath away, her beauty would have done so. There was little time to fall in love though, for already the princess had opened her lovely eyes, and was about to open her lovely mouth to scream at the sight of the wolf. Swiftly the wolf took hold of the princess's sleeping robe in his teeth, plucked her out of bed, and on to his back, in front of Ivan. Then out through the window he bounded, across the courtyard and over the moat, before her cries could rouse the castle sentinels. Princess Helen wept on the way back to Czar Afron's palace, and though Ivan tried to comfort her, he too could not bear the idea of her being married to the

ugly and impatient Czar. In fact before they were half way there, he and the princess had decided they would far rather be married to each other.

"What about the golden-maned horse?" asked the wolf, when Ivan had explained that he could not give up the princess to the Czar. "How will you obtain the Firebird without it?"

"Neither the golden-maned horse nor the Firebird itself is worth one single hair of my princess's head," said Ivan. "Helen shall come home with me, even if I must fail in my quest."

"Well spoken," said the wolf, "and no man has ever made a wiser choice, if I may say so" he added, with an arch glance at the princess. "You are, however," he continued, "the son of your father, and must still do his bidding. Allow me to be of further assistance." Ivan replied that the wolf had already done more than his fair share, but the agreeable animal silenced his protests with a raised paw. "Czar Afron awaits a beauteous princess and he shall receive one. I shall change myself—with little effort, I assure you—into the living image

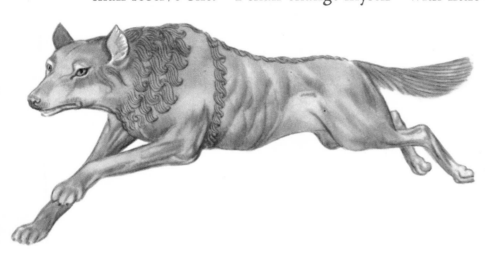

of Princess Helen. You, Ivan, may present me to the Czar in that guise and receive your horse." They left the real Princess Helen beneath the shelter of a large oak tree, and shortly afterwards Ivan returned. leading the horse with the golden mane. Once inside the palace the wolf, it seemed, had indeed turned into an exact likeness of Princess Helen. The testy Czar had been well satisfied with this wolf in ladies' clothing, and had promptly given Ivan the horse. As he and Helen rode away together on the magnificent steed Ivan could not help feeling a trifle sad at leaving the wolf behind. But they had scarcely reached the gates of Czar Dolmat's palace where the Firebird was, when the wolf, back to his customary shape, came up with them.

"All was well until the Czar caught my reflection in one of the palace mirrors," he gasped. "Mirrors always show the truth of course, and he saw through my princess disguise at once. "Good heavens, what a very plain young woman you are after all!" he cried, (I suppose my wolf's face did look rather dreadful in that fetching hat of yours, my dear Helen). Anyway he told me to go back to the Steppes and went into one of his dreadful rages. I don't mind telling you, I'm extremely glad to have escaped from them." Czar Dolmat received the horse, and Ivan the Firebird in a fireproof cage. How the wolf carried them all home is a mystery, but then he *was* a rather remarkable animal.

Ivan's father was delighted—if somewhat surprised—that his youngest son had captured the Firebird. He treated Ivan with a new respect, and proclaimed publicly that the young man should be heir to all his great estates.

"There's nothing for it," said Dimitri to Vassily. "The shame of being bested by our little brother is too much. I cannot stay here and bear it."

"He's not so little any more," replied Vassily. "The scoundrel has suddenly grown up behind our backs, and is soon to be married and settled. It's a disgrace, that's what it is!"

"Truly, but the disgrace is ours," said Dimitri. "We must join the army at once." So they put on their heaviest armour and went. And everybody managed to get on well enough without them.

Ivan married his Helen and the Czar gave them one of his finest castles to live in. When in time Ivan became Czar himself, he ruled wisely; for in seeking the Firebird he had found the importance of fair exchange. And as honesty is the best policy, his kingdom prospered.

Everybody was content with their lot, especially the Firebird, who now had an exclusive diet of golden apples and was far more agreeable in consequence—hardly ever going up in smoke again.

As for the wolf, he went to live with Helen and Ivan in the luxury of their grand home. He was a great favourite with the two small princes and one princess who joined them there as time went by. In fact the wolf became quite as tame as any household dog. Indeed for all we know, he may well have been the very first wolf hound.

The Tale of
The Doll

The doll was no smooth-complexioned beauty, being carved from a block of plain wood, with yellow twists of wool for hair. Nevertheless Natasha treasured it ; for the toy had been her mother's parting gift, and was all Natasha had to remember her by. The mother had died when Natasha was very small, but even now that she had passed her sixteenth birthday, the doll went with her everywhere.

Natasha's father was a merchant, and on one of his journeys to the big city, he met a widow with two daughters and decided to marry again. So Natasha found that she had two stepsisters as well as a stepmother, who, (when the merchant was away) treated her most un-kindly. You see, the stepmother's own daughters were clumsy creatures without any sort of charm, while Natasha had grown into a lively and attractive young woman. The contrast was so great that the stepmother took to shutting Natasha (and her attractions) indoors to do the scrubbing and rubbing, in the hope of turning her into a worn drab. But Natasha's cheeks grew brighter from the glow of the stove, her waist trimmer from stooping to clean the floors, while the two lazy sisters sat lumpishly about watching her work. Consequently all the gentlemen who were invited to call fell in love at once with Natasha, in her shabby smock, and spared not a glance for the other girls. The stepmother decided that she must rid herself of Natasha, unless her own daughters were to become old maids. Waiting until the merchant had left on a long trip, the bad stepmother called the three girls together and set them each a task. Her own daughters were to crotchet and knit, while Natasha was to spin. She kept them at their tasks until twilight when Natasha asked if she might have a candle.

" Certainly not," snapped the stepmother. " We have no fire in the house from which to light one, coals being the price they are ! "

" *I'm* not troubled," drawled the first stepdaughter, " for a fair light comes from my steel crochet hook."

" Nor *I*," yawned the second stepdaughter. " My steel needles give me enough light." Natasha however was in danger of running the spindle through her finger, and could not continue her work.

" Go then," said the stepmother, " and fetch a flaming torch from the witch of the forest. She always keeps a fire burning under her cauldron, I'm told. Then we shall light as many candles as you wish."

" Be off," said the ungracious sisters, and they hustled Natasha towards the door so

quickly that she only just had time to pick up her doll from the settle, on the way out. The stepmother and the sisters bolted the door behind her and joined hands in a gleeful dance, for they knew there would not be much hope for Natasha, once she fell into the gnarled hands of the witch.

The forest was dark and unfriendly, and Natasha might have been dreadfully afraid, but for the doll. Somehow the creature's painted eyes seemed to shine encouragingly in the gloom, and its wooden hand felt warm and comforting in her own palm. Natasha walked on through the forest until the pale dawn began to show through the network of branches above her head. There came the hollow clatter of horses hooves, and past Natasha swept a white rider, on a white horse with white saddle and reins. She stepped back abruptly, shivering, for the air was cool in the rider's wake and held more firmly to the hand of the wooden doll.

A while later the sun flushed over the horizon and with it came another horseman, dressed all in red, his horse a strawberry roan, saddled in scarlet leather. It was warmer presently, and Natasha curled up in a sun-lapped dell to rest, clutching her doll. Dusk had descended and the atmosphere was chill, before she awoke. As Natasha started again on her way, hold-ing the doll tight to her for warmth, she saw a third horseman, dressed entirely in black from the top of his fur hat to the tip of his well-shone leather boots. He cracked a jet whip and his dark steed leaped upwards and over a high fence that stood on the outskirts of the forest. Suddenly Natasha could see no more, for darkness had again descended. If it had not been for the re-assuring feeling of the doll's smooth shape, the poor girl would have lost all her courage. She stumbled on though, and ahead there came a glimmer of flame from the other side of the trees, where the black rider had disappeared.

"That must be the fire of the forest witch," thought Natasha, and found her way to the fence over which the dark horse had bounded. Out of the trees it was light enough to see that there was a gateway in the fence, and Natasha lifted the bar and walked through. Within was a house facing a stone courtyard. In the centre of the yard blazed a huge fire. On it a black cauldron boiled busily. Natasha approached hesitantly and knocked at the door of the house. It was opened by a very old lady with hair that stuck up sharply on all sides about her head like spun white sugar. Her teeth and her nails were long and sharp too, and so was her tongue, as Natasha learned :

"What do you mean by coming here, impertinent wench? I am the witch of the forest, and not to be trifled with by any little flibbertigibbet who cares to call."

"Indeed not, ma'am," stammered Natasha. "I should far rather not have disturbed you, to be sure. Yet I am sent by my stepmother to ask for the loan of a flame for our candle."

"Loan?" repeated the witch incredulously. "I never lend anybody anything. On the contrary, *they* usually lend themselves to me. And that is what you shall do, having chosen my doorstep for your begging." With that she took hold of Natasha with her scratchy fingers and dragged her indoors.

Inside, the witch surveyed the trembling girl a trifle less severely. "Do my bidding, child, and you shall have your flame," she said. "And don't stand there shaking so. It quite gives me a turn. I shan't do any harm, provided you are good, obedient and make yourself thoroughly useful about the place, rest assured."

It seemed that the witch was not quite as wicked as she looked, and Natasha, tucking the doll safely into a deep pocket in her dress, set about trying to please her.

"You will sweep the floors, and the courtyard, and the chimney and all the cupboards inside out," said the witch. "Then there is the washing and ironing. And in your spare time you may husk the grain in the kneading-trough. See that it is all done properly when I return in the morning, or I shall be obliged to change you into something useful—a beetle perhaps for tomorrow's dinner. They lend a nice flavour you know, to a bat casserole." Natasha shuddered and began her chores hastily, hoping that she would never be asked to try the flavour, and the witch flew off on her broomstick into the night.

Needless to say Natasha had no sleep, but toiled away until she saw in the pale dawn

through the window, the same white rider of yesterday, bringing his horse over the fence into the courtyard. The rider led his steed to some stables at the back of the witch's house, and Natasha bent again to her tasks. She had not yet managed to husk the grain in the kneading-trough, though the house was clean and neat, when the witch came back.

"Well girl, have you yet swept the floor?"

"Yes ma'am," said Natasha.

"And the courtyard and the chimney and all the cupboards inside out?" demanded the witch. Natasha said that she had. "The washing hangs out on the line fresh and sweet," she added anxiously. "And your linen is starched and ironed to perfection." All the time Natasha was dreading that the witch would ask about the grain in the kneading-trough, and of course this was the witch's next question.

"Come child, don't dilly dally. Show me the grain that you have husked, and we shall say no more of beetles in the stew or bats in the belfry or anything else that upsets you."

Natasha accompanied the witch reluctantly to the kneading-trough, knowing quite well that none of the grain had been husked. She wished herself a thousand miles away, as the witch raised the lid of the trough and peered inside. But instead of a cry of fury, the witch gave a cry of delight, because each and every morsel of grain had been neatly husked, just as she had wanted.

Then Natasha knew that her doll was enchanted, and had been protecting her all this while with its magic powers. They must have been stronger powers than those of the witch herself. For who else could have husked the grain in so short a moment but a magic doll. And, come to think of it, who else could have brought her safely through the forest to the very door of the witch's house?

The witch was so pleased that she gave Natasha a burning torch from the fire under her cauldron, and said she might go back home.

"I shall send my three horsemen to ride alongside until you are clear of the trees," promised the witch. "Who knows what dangers lurk there?"

"You really aren't a bad old witch after all, as witches go" said Natasha. "But I already have something to protect me, you see. However, I should like to know who these strange horsemen are, ma'am."

"Then you shall," said the witch briskly. "The rider all in white is he who heralds the dawn. The red rider brings the sunrise; and as for the horseman clad in black, he is the harbinger of night. They are my faithful servants, for a witch must have power over light and darkness."

With the aid of the burning torch Natasha had no trouble in finding her way back through the forest, and reached home the following morning, very tired, but none the worse for her adventure.

The stepmother and sisters were surprised and also dismayed to find that Natasha had returned safely from the witch of the forest, having hoped and expected never to see her again.

They had to pretend to be pleased though, and the stepmother made a great show of lighting the fire with the flaming torch so that Natasha might warm herself. As it turned out, the fire warmed the stepmother and her homely daughters instead, for, no matter how far away from it they stood, the flames would lick out every now and again and give them a stinging burn.

"The fire is bewitched," screamed the stepmother. "We must escape at once." Picking up their skirts with cries of confusion the three fled back to the big city as fast as their heavy feet would carry them. Natasha could not say that she was sorry to see them go, and thought privately that perhaps her father would not miss them so very much either. For the stepmother had not been a kind and dutiful wife.

All the same Natasha found the house quiet and lonely, for though the doll had proved to be an excellent companion on her adventures, it was not the talkative kind.

She was more than usually pleased therefore to greet the lady who knocked at the door with the washing, a day or so later.

"Come in and rest yourself," Natasha invited her warmly, and the washerwoman was glad to do so. "A charming place you have here," she smiled. "Very different from my own little room, up in the attic of Petrov the Cobbler."

"Stay and keep me company then," said Natasha, for the washerwoman was a kindly and comfortable person. "You shall put a rouble of rent in your own pocket, instead of in old Petrov's, for a change." The washerwoman said she would be happy to agree, but only on condition that Natasha allowed her to do all the housework. "Those little hands are toilworn enough, my dear, for one so young and lovely. That stepmother of yours has used you most shabbily, shame on her!" The good soul waited on her so devotedly that Natasha felt she would grow as lazy as her departed stepsisters unless she found some useful occupation. The stepmother had taken all her clothes and jewels to the big city, but had been unable to carry a pile of best quality flax, intended for a gown. Natasha found it, and sat at the spinning-wheel, the doll propped up as usual beside her, spinning the flax into thread as fine and silky as hair. Then she wove the thread, on her loom, into a delicate material, soft, and tenuous as a cobweb. When the washerwoman saw the cloth she said:

"I do declare, there's magic in your fingers, my girl, and no mistake. Why, this material is fit for royalty, and this very day I shall take it to the Czar!" The washerwoman had often been to the palace, and was quite one of the Czar's favourite workers, for she crisped his cuffs and pressed his pleats as nobody else could. She had no difficulty there-

fore in gaining an audience with the mighty man, who examined the material with interest.

"Exquisite!" he pronounced. "Where my good woman did you find a cloth of so fine a texture? I must have twelve shirts made of it at once!" The washerwoman curtseyed low. "If it please you, lord, and I can see well enough it does, a young lady of my acquaintance has woven it with her own fair hands."

"Then she shall make my shirts," pronounced the Czar, and the washerwoman informed him that Natasha would be honoured. She was too, when she heard, and ran to fetch the doll and her keen scissors. Sitting the doll on a table, and spreading out the material, Natasha began to cut out the shirts. But the material was so gossamer thin that it began to fall apart at the touch of the sharp blades, much to Natasha's distress.

"I cannot make the Czar's shirts," she wailed. "And he has put his trust in me."

"Come, don't fret," said the washerwoman. "Go to bed and finish your work in the morning."

"I cannot," repeated Natasha dismally, but she went to bed, leaving her doll on the table near the material. Next morning of course the clever doll had put everything right with a little well applied magic, for there on the table were twelve shirts, beautifully cut from the fragile material, and ready sewn. Natasha looked from the doll to the shirts and again to the doll, who stared back blankly, as if nothing out of the ordinary had occurred at all during the night. This innocence did not deceive Natasha though, and she hugged and kissed her faithful toy until its painted face was quite damp. "Dear wonderful doll," she sighed. "How could I ever manage without you?"

For the first time in all the years Natasha had had the doll, it actually spoke! "You'll manage without me well enough from now on, child, just wait and see. My work is

done and I'm leaving now, for your doll playing days are over." Natasha was so astonished that she dropped it. Whereupon the doll rose on its wooden legs and, walking stiffly as if on stilts, went out through the front door. It turned once, waved a jointed arm, and then stumped away into the distance.

"I never did!" exclaimed the washer-woman, who had witnessed the scene. "I never did, really I never!" Natasha wiped away a tear. "Neither did I," she said,

" nor anyone else either."

The washerwoman took Natasha to the Czar, so that she might have the pleasure of presenting the twelve perfect shirts to him herself. It was hard to tell which pleased the Czar most—the beautiful shirts or the beautiful face of Natasha as she curtseyed, with modest pride, before him.

" Exquisite," murmured the Czar (could he have meant the shirts or the slim shape of Natasha as she rose to kiss his hand?). " Young woman, I am most impressed."

Natasha blushed and said that she was delighted to have been of service, and would there be anything else required?

" Indeed there would," replied the Czar unexpectedly. " I require your presence tonight at a banquet here in the palace—that is, of course, if you would care to come? "

Natasha cared very much indeed, for the Czar had a handsome face and kindly ways. He would doubtless make a charming dining companion, and it was not every day that a girl was invited to a royal banquet, after all. She accepted gracefully and went home with the washerwoman in high spirits.

Fortunately Natasha did have one really fine ball gown, a present from her father before he had re-married. The stepmother had never allowed her to go out in it, so the dress was as good as new, if not entirely fashionable. When the washerwoman had finished doing up all the buttons and bows, and stood back to see the effect, she pronounced that Natasha looked lovelier than ever, fashionable or not. It was clear when she arrived at the palace that the Czar cared little for fashion either, for he had no eyes for anyone except Natasha. During the banquet she sat at his side, and the Czar had asked her never to leave it, even before the dessert.

And even before the coffee and brandy, Natasha had decided to accept. It was not a hard decision to make, for actually she had fallen in love with the Czar the very first time they met, and he with her.

At the end of the meal the Czar stood up and announced the engagement, and a toast was drunk to the happy pair.

Soon Natasha was to possess not one ball gown but one hundred, and a different set of jewels to match each of them. For the Czar delighted in showering her with gifts, and no girl in the land had a finer trousseau. How jealous the stepmother and her daughters were when they heard of Natasha's good fortune. And how they wished they had treated her more kindly in order to share it.

The wedding took place without delay, and when the merchant returned from his journey, he was most gratified to find that, in the meantime, his daughter had become a Czarina. He was also secretly rather pleased to be able to call his home his own again, now that the strict stepmother had left him in peace. The washerwoman became his housekeeper, and there was no brighter, cleaner or more cheerful establishment to be seen in the district, unless it was the royal palace.

As for Natasha: although she missed her doll, the new Czarina no longer needed it. For in a while the most powerful magic of all occurred, and she had a real live doll of her own to mother and pet.

The Tale of
Simple Simeon

They called him simple, but really Simeon was only a trifle slow. True, his two brothers were bright and industrious, while Simeon was content to spend most of his days sleeping above the stove. But actually Simeon was a good deal less foolish than he appeared to be, as you shall hear.

The brothers told Simeon one day : " The time has come to rouse yourself, my lad, for we are to spend the winter away from home, on business."

" Then *you* must rouse yourselves, not I," observed Simeon drowsily. " And the best of good fortune to you, brothers."

" Care for our wives while we are gone," said the brothers, " and you shall have a red cloak, a red cap and a pair of red boots, when summer comes." These Simeon desired more than anything else in the world, so he sat up eagerly, and promised to do his best. And his best turned out a deal better than usual, because he wanted to do it, you see. . . .

When the husbands had departed, their wives, who had often teased and scolded Simeon for his laziness, now found him to be an excellent man-of-the-house. They were able to go out and about frequently, for the water pail was always full, fresh fish arrived each day from the stream to fill the larder, and piles of wood lay ready to make the fires. Yet strangely enough, Simeon hardly ever troubled himself, and indeed still remained for most of the time stretched out dozily on the stove.

The first day of the brothers absence, Simeon had ventured out, however, to fetch the water and catch some fish. The lake was frosted over with thin ice, and the fish could be seen darting about beneath, as if in a green glass aquarium. One large chap—a pike—particularly caught Simeon's eye, and making a hole in the ice he waited. Soon the pike swam across the hole and deftly Simeon put his arm into the cold water and grasped it. Wriggling and gaping helplessly the fish was drawn upwards and out. Simeon met its pleading gaze sympathetically, for he was a kindly boy. " Sorry to put you out, poor fish," he apologised.

" Then having put me out, put me back again," suggested the fish, breathing hard. " That is if you're really sorry, and not codding."

" It's not codding I'm at but *piking*," replied Simeon, unperturbed. " The wives must have a fish to fry for their supper, or I shan't receive the red cloak, red cap and red boots when

my brothers come home."

"There's more in life than a pair of boots," said the fish rather limply. "I'll do far better for you than that, if you spare my life. This fresh air will be the death of me before long!"

"What will you do for me?" asked Simeon cautiously.

"All your work, for a start," promised the pike, almost at its last gasp.

"That's a bargain," replied Simeon, and returned the fish to the water. "Now don't forget your promise," he shouted down through the hole in the ice.

"Not I," said the pike, catching his breath blissfully. "We fish never talk unless we mean what we say. Now, if there's anything I can do, you have only to call: 'By power of fish, and by my wish'—and it will be done."

"I hardly know how to thank you," said Simeon.

"Your servant sir," answered the fish, and turning tail, dipped under the ice and swam away.

Simeon filled his pails with water and found that they were extremely heavy to lift.

"By power of fish, and by my wish," he exclaimed, "buckets, take yourselves home, for I'll not carry you!" The buckets began to slither and slide along the ice, much to the astonishment of passers-by, bumped over the bank and tumbled down the hill in the direction of Simeon's home. They arrived even before he did, without spilling a drop of water, and stacked themselves tidily beneath the sink, ready for use.

Then Simeon shouldered his axe and went to fetch the sledge. "By power of fish, and by my wish—sledge, bring the wood!" The sledge shot off unaided across the snow, and the axe jumped off Simeon's shoulder and hopped on its handle, like a man with a wooden leg, in fast pursuit. Simeon sat down and watched them disappear towards the forest. A while later the sledge returned with a load of wood, neatly chopped by the axe, which had buried itself in the top log for the ride.

So this was how Simeon managed to do all the household chores without bestirring himself unduly. Within a week the little village was alive with gossip, for many people had seen the buckets bouncing across the ice each morning, and many more had been in danger of injury from a wildly careering sledge, with no driver, on its daily trip to the woods.

"That foolish Simeon," said the villagers. "There's no knowing what he'll be up to next, for the boy hasn't an ounce of sense."

"Deserves a good thrashing," said others, rubbing their shoulders and shins, which had come into sharp contact with the buckets or the sledge. "We'll teach him to try his trickery on us !'' Arming themselves with some stout sticks, the men of the village and some of the women too, went to Simeon's house and dragged him outside.

"By power of fish, and by my wish—,'' cried Simeon, arms upraised to shield himself from the blows, "sticks, beat the beaters !'' At once the sticks jumped out of the villagers' hands and dealt each of them a resounding whack. The mob released Simeon and fled in terror, the sticks jumping along behind, with a sharp tap here and there, to help them on their way.

The villagers went on gossiping, but now they spoke of Simeon with new esteem. Even the wives finally noticed that their housework was being performed in a most unusual way, for arriving home early one day they were amazed to see Simeon sitting idly by in the yard, while his axe busily chopped wood without any help at all ! From that moment on they too treated Simeon not as a simple boy, but as a very special and important person indeed.

The news of his fame reached the ears of the old Czar himself. The Czar had lived a long time and thought he knew everything ; but even he had never known an axe that did its own chopping, or a sledge its own sleighing, or buckets their own bringing.

"I must see these wonders for myself,'' he announced. "Have this Simple Simeon brought to me.'' A soldier of the guard was sent to Simeon's house. Simeon had been having a quiet nap on the stove, and was not pleased to be disturbed by the soldier's impatient knock. He made his way slowly to the door, opened it, and peered at the officer sleepily :

"How can I help you, sir ? '' he yawned. "Come, make haste and tell me, there's a good fellow, for it is cold and draughty here in the doorway.'' The soldier glowered at him.

"Let me in then, Simple Simeon, for I am come by royal command of the Czar. And it does not do, my lad, to keep the Czar waiting, I can tell you!" he said crossly. Simeon opened the door unwillingly, and allowed the soldier to enter. "Don't stay too long, I beg," he said. "You have interrupted my favourite dream in which I am striding along Red Square in the great city—and to match the square I wear a red cloak, a red cap and a red pair of boots. What do you think of that for splendour, hey soldier?"

"An officer of the Czar has no time for idle dreams," retorted the soldier impatiently. "I came here to command your immediate presence at the palace. Any delay will doubtless result in the loss of your head— which would be no great loss to you of course, your head being entirely empty!"

"It is cold outside, and you will hardly make a pleasant companion," Simeon told the soldier. I shall not come, so kindly be off and leave me in peace."

"You would dare to disobey the Czar?" spluttered the soldier. "Now see here, I have an order, and an order must be obeyed. You'll accompany me, willing or not, and pay your respects to my master." Roughly, he took hold of Simeon and shoved him towards his own horse-sleigh waiting outside. Simeon climbed across the shafts of the sleigh, behind the horse, and sat surveying the soldier, with his feet spread apart and his arms folded.

"You must know, sir, that I only do those things that I wish to do. And I only wish to do things when spoken to kindly. You have not spoken to me kindly, therefore I shall not do as *you* wish, but as *I* wish. By power of fish, and by *my* wish—horse, disappear!" Before the soldier's horrified gaze, his horse immediately vanished from its harness, leaving the heavy sleigh without any means of motion. "Here!" called the soldier, "you'll not get away with that, young rascal. Bring back my horse this instant." He ran towards the sledge intending to punish Simeon for his impertinence.

"By power of fish, and by my wish—sleigh, chase him away!" shouted Simeon. The sleigh began suddenly to move forward towards the soldier, its shafts pointing at his chest. Faster and faster it came, Simeon still sitting astride, and the soldier turned and ran for his life. Simeon and the sleigh chased him all the way back to the Czar's palace; and then Simeon wished to be taken home.

The Czar was furious when the soldier

recounted his story. "You have handled the matter clumsily," he remarked, "and, it seems, have already been justly punished for your ill-manners." Indeed the soldier had not yet recovered from his frightening experience with the sleigh. He looked pale and was trembling in a most unsoldierly way. It was clear that he was no longer fit to serve the Czar, and received his dismissal from the guards, there and then.

As a result of the soldier's tale, the Czar was more anxious than ever to meet Simeon, who could not be half so simple as he had been led to believe. This time, instead of sending an uncouth soldier, the Czar commanded his chief counsellor to bring Simeon before him. The counsellor arrived next day at Simeon's house, and his knock, like the soldier's, woke Simeon from his nap on top of the stove. He opened the door none too gladly, rubbing the sleep from his eyes. It appeared that the counsellor, like the soldier, had interrupted Simeon's favourite dream—the one about the red cap and red cloak and red boots. He told the counsellor all about it, and the wise man listened with interest.

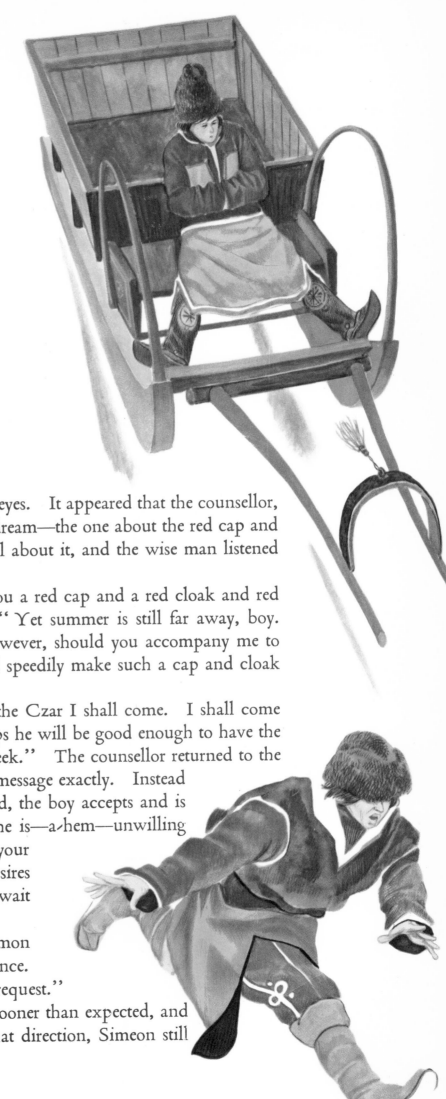

"You say that your brothers have promised you a red cap and a red cloak and red boots when winter is past," said the counsellor. "Yet summer is still far away, boy. You will have a long wait for your treasures. However, should you accompany me to the Czar, I don't doubt that the palace tailor could speedily make such a cap and cloak and boots."

"In that case," said Simeon, "you may tell the Czar I shall come. I shall come in my own time and my own way though. Perhaps he will be good enough to have the clothes ready and awaiting my arrival within the week." The counsellor returned to the Czar, but he was far too tactful to repeat Simeon's message exactly. Instead he said, bowing low : "May it please you my lord, the boy accepts and is honoured by your gracious invitation. However he is—a-hem—unwilling to enter the palace without a costume worthy of your esteemed presence. In short—a-hem—the boy desires a red cap, a red cloak and a pair of red boots, to await his arrival within the week."

"It shall be done," said the Czar. "Summon my tailor. The garments are to be fashioned at once. Inform the boy that I have graciously agreed to his request."

Although he was to receive his heart's desire sooner than expected, and no longer relied upon his brothers' generosity in that direction, Simeon still used his magic powers to help the wives with their household tasks. They now held Simeon in great awe, and allowed him to remain cosily on the stove as long as he chose, dreaming his dreams and whiling the hours away. Nearly a week passed, and on the sixth day Simeon awoke and said : " By power of fish and by my wish—stove, take me to the Czar's palace." The wives threw up their hands in alarm, for the walls around them and the ground underfoot began to shake and shudder. There came a grinding, tearing noise, and the air was suddenly full of dust and mortar, as the stove tore itself out of the hearth. With Simeon still lying easily on top, the stove floated slowly and majestically out through the door of the house, down the road past several startled wayfarers, and all the way to the palace of the Czar. When the sentries saw it coming, they lowered their muskets and opened the gates ; for they had received orders from the Czar himself to let Simeon in. Up the marble stairs and into the Czar's own chamber drifted the stove, and set itself down at the royal gentleman's feet. The counsellors, one and all, flocked around, staring unbelievingly at Simeon, who was so warm and comfortable that he refused to move from the stove's top, even for the Czar.

It happened, just at that moment, that the Czar's only granddaughter, lovely Princess Tamara, passed by the window and saw the extraordinary scene. Her curiosity aroused by the young man on the stove, she stopped and stared in a most unroyal manner. Simeon

looked back at her, and quite suddenly he opened his eyes wider than ever before, sat up with a jerk, and for once looked thoroughly lively. Gone was the casual air and the sleepy expression. No more the lazy, sprawling attitude that had made people consider him stupid. Simeon had been awakened you see, by love for the Princess Tamara, and because of it he became at once what he ought to have been all along—a smart active young man with a head full of the most beautiful thoughts. And the beautiful thoughts shone from his face, making him so handsome that Princess Tamara knew too that she had found her beloved.

The royal tailor entered the room, and the Czar said to Simeon. " My good fellow, the wonder we have witnessed today certainly merits this red cap and red cloak and red boots. May you wear them well." Simeon did not take his glance from the princess. " Sir," he replied. " I know now that these things are not my true heart's desire. For my heart has, in a single moment, changed, and the rest of me with it. So keep the red cap, red cloak and red boots, if it please you my lord Czar, and give me in marriage that ravishing maiden who stands at the window."

Princess Tamara blushed pink with pleasure, but the Czar blushed purple with fury. " That, you insolent pup, happens to be my own granddaughter, the Princess Tamara ! " he roared. " With every prince and potentate in the land clamouring for her hand, do you think she would look at you, a nobody from nowhere ? "

" Everybody is a somebody from somewhere," pointed out Simeon calmly, " and the princess *is* looking at me, this very minute, you'll observe. Not unfavourably either, I dare to hope and pray."

"How *dare* you dare?" thundered the Czar. "This audacity will cost your life, scoundrel!" At this point the princess came in through the door and approached the Czar.

"Come grandfather, don't be old-fashioned. Allow me to choose my own husband. You do want me to be happy really and truly? I should be with this young man, I know I should." She stroked her grandfather's white beard coaxingly. The Czar had never learned how to stay angry for very long with the pretty princess. In a while the high colour had left his face, and his mouth twitched slightly, as if he were trying hard not to smile. "Always has been impossible to refuse you, little witch," the Czar said at last, in quite another tone of voice. "You may as well marry this Simeon as another man, I suppose. For none of them is good enough for my Tamara, in her grandfather's failing eyes, as well she knows."

At this Simeon jumped down from the stove and fell on one knee before the old Czar. "Sir, you will never regret it, for I have power to watch over the princess all the days of her life. We thank you for your blessings."

Simeon sent the stove home without him, for he had not time for it any more now that he had met the princess. There was far too much to think about and talk about, in preparation for the grand wedding which the Czar intended to give them. The great day seemed long in arriving but at last it did. Simeon and the princess were married in splendour, and after the ceremony the Czar held a huge banquet in their honour, to which all the local dignit-

aries and royal personages were invited. Among the guests were several of the princes whom Tamara had turned down in favour of Simeon, and they gathered together in a mean little group, whispering jealously.

"What has this upstart to offer the most desirable princess in all Russia?" hissed one prince, who was very rich and nasty. "By all accounts he has some sort of fool's luck," muttered another, "for I hear his behaviour is somewhat strange."

"Let's rid ourselves of him," said the rich and nasty one. "We'd be doing the Czar a favour, and the princess too, if only she knew it." They put their princely heads closer together and began to hatch a plot, there and then at the wedding, for the downfall of Simeon. One of the princes slipped away to the apothecary shop, and came back with a packet of special sleeping powder, which he put into a glass of wine intended for the bridegroom. No sooner had Simeon drunk the draught than he fell down as if dead. The guests stared in horror, and Princess Tamara screamed and wept most pitifully, but nothing could rouse Simeon. He slept more soundly than he had done on top of the stove, in the days when sleep was more important to him than anything, except a red cap, a red cloak and red boots. The rich and nasty prince took Simeon by the head, and the one who had drugged his wine took him by the feet, and they carried the still body upstairs to the state bedroom. As soon as the door was closed behind them, the princes shut the sleeping Simeon up in a cask, which had been put there in readiness, by another of the schemers. Then flinging wide the casement, the two villains strainingly lifted the cask and dropped it—and Simeon —down into the murky moat. The moat flowed out under a low bridge into a sluggish stream ; the stream led to a rapidly flowing river and the cask was swept along it. The princes thought they were well rid of Simeon, and closing the casement, went home to celebrate. Certainly if Simeon had gone on sleeping he would have used what little air remained in the cask, and died. However, having had more rest during his life than most others, the sleeping draught did not act quite so strongly upon him as it was intended to. Stirring, he opened his eyes, peered hazily into the gloom and discovered that he could hardly breath. "By power of fish, and my own wish" he called desperately, "show me the light, before I perish!" As Simeon spoke the lid of the cask flew open and a rush of cool air revived him. He struggled to a standing position and found himself face to face with the very pike who had been so kind and helpful in the past. The pike was head and tail out of the water, and surveyed him glassily. Simeon drew several deep breaths and said :

" Now I know how you felt that day on the ice. It's as bad to be a man out of air as a fish out of water."

" I think I know what you mean," said the pike, diving down for a breather and surfacing again to continue the conversation. " None of us is at an advantage out of our element. I can see you have not fared well, my friend, even with the magic powers."

" All was well enough," said Simeon, " until the night of my wedding. Yes, good pike, I had found myself a beautiful princess to marry, and gained the high opinion even of the Czar himself, with your help. But now my enemies have the better of me, and here I am marooned in the middle of the ocean instead of being with my adorable wife. Who knows if I shall ever see her again, for goodness knows where we are now, probably a thousand miles away."

" It happens that I know the seas like the back of my tail, though goodness is not how I should actually describe myself," said the pike, with touching modesty. " In fact, dear fellow, you are indeed far from your loved one, who, I should not be at all surprised, is at this moment bemoaning your loss most bitterly. On the other hand there are some surrounding her who are not sorry at all to think you are drowned, and hope that the princess will now marry one of them instead. You had better return as fast as you know how, my boy."

" That's the trouble, I don't know how," said Simeon. " I'm all at sea again, and can't think quite clearly for the moment. Someone must have put some sleeping medicine in my wine that night."

" Then I'll refresh your memory," said the pike. " By the power of fish and by my wish, cask—take Simeon back to his wife with all possible speed."

The pike dived downwards with a farewell flick of his tail towards Simeon, and the cask began to thrash through the water at tremendous speed, back in the direction of the palace. Down the river, along the stream and under the bridge it whirled, into the palace moat. Tamara was there on the causeway, looking mournfully out across the water, surrounded by the wicked princes. They were pretending to console her, smiling behind their hands at

each other, the while. The cask brought Simeon to port with such a rush that everyone was quite drenched with spray. Princess Tamara did not mind getting wet though, for the husband she had given up for lost came running up the steps of the causeway, and into her outstretched arms.

When the princes saw that Simeon had not been drowned after all, and that they were found out, the wretches fell on their knees begging for mercy.

" I shall not have you punished," said Simeon, who was now wide awake again, " but look on my power, and know that never again am I to be trifled with." He raised his arms and intoned: "By power of fish and by my wish—castle, rise out of the earth." As he spoke, on the other side of the moat a wonderful palace appeared, twelve turrets high and inlaid with the finest gold and rubies. "Here is our married home, dear wife," he told Tamara, as the princes watched in awe. "Nobody shall say that I cannot provide for my wife as well as the next man." And after that nobody did say so, for it was clear that Simeon was simple no more.

The Tale of The Frog Princess

There was a Czar with three bachelor sons, and he thought they should be married.

"You boys spend too much time hunting and fishing," the Czar admonished, "and not enough on seeking wives. Who will carry on our noble line, if none of you have sons?"

"By chance we have never found the Right Woman," said Prince Mischa, who had not actually looked much further than his long bow.

"Then, by chance, you shall all find her this very day," announced the Czar. "Mischa, Ilya and Sergei, take each an arrow and shoot it out of the casement window. The arrow must speed to your own true love, who will bring it back here. In this way you can tell the Right Woman when you see her."

"Supposing our own true love turns out to be a dairymaid or the wood-cutter's daughter?" objected Ilya. "I shouldn't care to marry beneath me."

"Nor are you likely to," said the Czar somewhat coldly. "No matter in what station of life she belongs, the girl who returns the arrow shall be your wife. I have decreed it, so do as you're told without further talk."

"Let me shoot first, if it pleases you father," said Sergei eagerly. He was fonder of the Czar than his brothers. Fitting an arrow to his bow, he opened the window wide and took aim.

"Wait your turn," said Ilya, pulling him roughly away. He was the eldest and disliked being shown up by Sergei. Aiming his own bow, he shot an arrow up and away into the far yonder.

"Out of the way, scrap," said Mischa, anxious also not to be outdone by his junior. He too shot an arrow out of the window, which sped for the horizon. At last Sergei was allowed to stand forward, and his arrow went singing away through the window, to come down wherever it might.

A day passed, and a messenger came to tell Prince Ilya that a young lady had called to see him, bearing one of his silver monogrammed arrows.

"How does she look?" asked Ilya anxiously. "I'm not at home to anyone in the least resembling a dairymaid or a woodcutter's daughter."

"You'll marry her whoever she is," insisted the Czar. As it happened, when the young lady with the arrow was shown in, Ilya was relieved to find that she resembled himself, more than anyone else, being a high-bred haughty princess with good prospects and a snobbish air. Naturally he fell in love with her directly, and agreed to be married as soon as the Czar wished.

Next day the messenger came upon them again to announce that yet another young lady had called at the palace, bearing an arrow marked with Prince Mischa's initials. On being ushered into the royal presence, it was clear that she too could claim to be a princess of the bluest blood, for her nose and cheeks were a mottled mauve, and her hand felt cold to the touch. Mischa, who was not a warm-hearted fellow, found that they had a good deal in common, and like his brother, agreed to be married whenever the Czar wished. Now everyone was anxious to see what sort of a bride Sergei's arrow had found, and they waited for several days before she arrived. But when the messenger came to say that someone had called to see the youngest prince, bearing his silver arrow, he stammered and seemed so upset that Sergei was thoroughly alarmed.

"How does she look, my wife-to-be?" asked Sergei nervously. "I cannot—no, dare not, say," gasped the messenger. "Only see for yourself, my lord." He backed hastily and went to fetch the caller.

It was far worse than anyone had expected, for who should enter the royal chamber but a female frog, emerald green and dripping with slime! In her mouth the frog carried an arrow which was unmistakably Sergei's, having a small " S " embossed on the tip, with a coronet above. There was no going back on the Czar's decree—not even the Czar could do that. The frog had brought Sergei's arrow, and Sergei must marry the frog.

The two elder brothers and their regal wives laughed so heartily at Sergei and the frog, that Sergei felt somehow drawn towards the creature, his companion in misfortune.

The Czar was horrified at the fate of his youngest and favourite son, but he ordered that the wedding of the three princes should take place that same night. "What has to be has to be, and we may as well get it over," he told Sergei, with a comforting pat on the shoulder.

After the threefold ceremony, Mischa and Ilya received all the congratulations, while Sergei sat forlorn in a corner, with his frog wife on a silver platter. Only the Czar had a kind word to say : " Never mind my boy—your brothers' wives may not seem so super-ior tomorrow. For I intend to put these princesses to a test. Perhaps they are more proud than practical, you know." Accordingly next day the Czar proclaimed that his son's three wives should each sew him an embroidered tunic. The court was agog to see which of them would win the competition. Poor Sergei thought that his father's test would only serve to increase his own humili-ation—for how could a frog—even one with the best of intentions—ever hope to produce an embroidered tunic? Nevertheless he carried the scaly creature to his room on the silver platter, and set it down gently. He placed beside the frog the sewing materials and, after imploring the creature to do her best, went out to pace the battlements.

As soon as he was gone, the most extra-ordinary scene took place in the prince's room. The slimy skin fell away, and the frog turned into a beautiful princess with emerald green eyes and teeth like pearls. Clapping her smooth white hands, the princess called softly:

"Handmaidens, cast off your scales, and come to the aid of the Frog Princess!" Through the open window there came, with a hop, skip and a jump, six gleaming frogs. Leaving six thin trails of water behind them they approached the Frog Princess, sur-rounded her, and instantly changed into six curtsying handmaidens in sage-coloured smocks.

"What do you wish, Highness?" they inquired. And the princess asked them to show her how to make an embroidered tunic. "We must work quickly," she re-minded them, "for you know we have but an hour a day in our true form." They did work quickly, and within the hour a perfect tunic took form under their hands, and was complete. Then all at once the maidens disappeared, and six frogs hopped towards the window and out of it, bobbing briefly on the sill towards the princess. But she too was now froglike again, and had jumped back on the silver platter to await her husband's return.

When Sergei had finished his despairing walk on the battlements, he came back to his rooms and could hardly believe his eyes. For there beside the frog-wife was a faultless tunic, lavishly embroidered and neatly sewn. He looked intently at the frog but she was curled up on the silver platter, apparently fast asleep. Wrapping the tunic carefully, he put it near his bed. In the morning Sergei took the frog on her silver platter, and gave his father the parcel. Mischa's wife and Ilya's too had sat up most of the night working on their tunics. Yet being princesses, they had never had much occasion to do any sewing, and the results of their labours were two raggedy garments, hardly fit to wear. When the Czar opened Sergei's parcel and examined the frog's fine offering, he was delighted and proclaimed her the winner.

"It's not fair!" exclaimed the proud princesses. "That frog could never have made such a delicate tunic with her clumsy hands and feet. Give us another test, lord Czar, and we shall really show our worth."

"I dare say," remarked the Czar. "Very well, my son's three wives shall each cook me a loaf of bread. This competition ought finally to prove who is the best."

The two princesses put their haughty heads together and decided to keep watch on the frog. When Sergei had left her alone in the royal kitchens, the princesses opened the door slightly and peeped through. The frog seemed to be asleep on her silver platter, but actually she had one eye open and was aware that the princesses were spying on her. In a while the frog appeared to wake up, and hopping to the flour pot, upset it all over the kitchen table. Leaning on the water jug, she managed to pour some on to the pile of flour, and began kneading away with her webbed feet, until it was thick and gluey. Then the frog threw the hole sticky mess on to the fire and went back to sleep on her platter, evidently well satisfied with her work. The two princesses had never learned to cook, or to do anything else in the least

way useful for the matter of that, and they thought that this must be the ideal method to bake a loaf of bread. Which was just as the frog wished them to think. When Sergei had taken the frog back to his own room, the princesses entered the kitchen and did exactly as they had seen the frog do. Of course their loaves of bread, like the one the frog had pretended to make, were no better than scorched and blackened biscuits, and these they took to the Czar next day, more proudly than ever. They little guessed that in the middle of the night when Sergei was asleep the Frog Princess had called in her handmaidens. For an hour they had all thrown off their frog skins, crept down to the kitchen, and made a proper loaf of bread, which baked in the oven high and sweet as could be. Silently they had gone back to Sergei, placed the loaf by his bed and changed back into their froglike forms. The handmaidens returned to the pond and the frog Princess settled down on her silver platter to await the day.

The Czar received the three loaves of bread solemnly, and passed them round for the courtiers to taste. To the horror of Mischa and Ilya, the bread their wives had made was so hard and bitter that no one could swallow a morsel. Whereas, Sergei's loaf, made by the frog-wife, was crisp and delicious, and the Czar was only just able to capture a piece for himself before the courtiers finished it up entirely. "Superb!" he pronounced. "Sergei's wife is the winner beyond a doubt!"

The nose of the blue-blooded princess had turned from mauve to green with jealousy, and the high-and-mighty one tossed her head angrily and snapped:

"Very clever I'm sure, mistress frog. But there's one thing you can't do better than us —and that is, *dance*. Unless of course it's the polka, which goes: 'One, two, three, HOP,'" she added sarcastically. This made the courtiers chuckle and Sergei flush. "By all means hold a ball, father," he exclaimed rashly. "I'm not ashamed of my little frog-wife!" So the Czar ordered that a ball should be held the following week.

In spite of his brave words, Sergei did not in the least look forward to appearing at the ball with a frog for a partner, and spent most of the time in deepest gloom. "My brothers and their wives will have the laugh on me now, and no mistake," he moaned, head in hands. "They will make me into the court Fool." When the night of the ball arrived, however, the Frog Princess threw off the scaly disguise and stood before her husband, a lovely lady,

gorgeously dressed in satins and silks. At first Sergei was too astonished to speak, and could only stare enraptured at the graceful vision. Finally he found words and begged the Frog Princess to explain this remarkable change. In a soft musical voice, quite unlike the croaking tones of the frog, the princess told her story.

"It all started twenty years ago, on the day I was born, or soon after, you see. And in the usual way too, with a christening party. My mother wanted to invite the wicked witch with everyone else, for fear of offending her, but father would not hear of it. The wicked witch came to hear that the party had been given without her, and was

absolutely furious. She came shooting along to the palace on her broomstick, straight through the throne-room window to my father's feet.

"'So-o-o,' she said, 'so-o-o you've had your christening party without me. The wicked witch isn't good enough for you high and mighty folk, it seems. Just because you're a king you think you can step on the faces of us humble creatures no doubt.'

"'A spell on you!' shrieked the witch. 'King you were born and king you shall be —king of the frogs!' As she spoke, mother says, father began to puff out his chest and shrink and shrivel. His eyes started to bulge from his head and his face turned a sickly shade of green. Before them all he turned into a clumsy frog who hopped out of the window and away to find a pond.

"Mother screamed, ran to the cradle and picked me up. 'You shall not harm my child,' she cried, and I cried too in sympathy, though of course I knew nothing of what had occurred.

"'Frogs, all of you, frogs!' screamed the witch, and there and then mother and I, hopped off after my father. 'And so you will remain,' the witch shouted after us, 'until that frog child of yours grows up and finds a prince who will marry and keep her for twenty days and nights.' And this is the twentieth night that you and I have been married, dear Sergei. Now the witch's spell is broken and none of us will wear our frog's skin again."

As she finished the tale, the door of Sergei's room opened and in trooped the princess's family, and their retainers, not in the least froglike now, for they wore the rich clothes that had been theirs before the en-chantment. Surrounding the happy couple, they escorted them, in splendid procession, down to the ballroom. The other two princesses had put on all their feathers and finery, and looked like a pair of the proudest peacocks that ever strutted. They could hardly wait to see Sergei's shame when he entered the ballroom with a frog on his arm.

"His Highness Prince Sergei and the Frog Princess," announced the footman, and the doors were flung wide to reveal, no frog with Sergei, but a ravishingly beautiful girl, attended by six handmaidens and a grand assortment of friends and relations. A sigh of admiration swept through the crowded ballroom as Sergei presented his charming partner to the Czar. The princess curtsied and the Czar, overjoyed to find that his son was no longer married to a frog, said that she and Sergei should open the ball with the first dance. It was a huge honour and the brothers and their wives could hardly contain themselves with envy. When the snooty princesses joined the dance, they tried to copy the Frog Princess's elegant progress across the ballroom floor, in the hope of attracting as much praise. But the soles of their shoes seemed unaccountably to be covered with slime—it was just the kind that collects on the surface of a stagnant pool—and the proud princesses began to slip and slide. Abruptly their feet shot from under them altogether, and the princesses hit the floor in a most undignified way, bringing Mischa and Ilya down with them! How everyone laughed! Sergei had to hold his sides; and as for the Czar, tears of mirth streamed down his face at the ridiculous sight.

That was the end of the princesses' pride, for the fall had knocked it right out of them. And the end too of the Tale of the Frog Princess.

The Tale of
Maria Marina

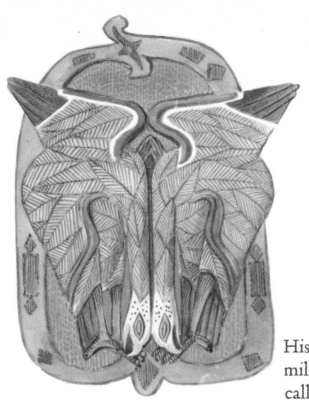

His name was Prince Vladimir Nikolai Andrei Maximillian Roskatov, Czar of the Four Rivers : but we shall call him Vava for short, because he was quite young and unassuming really. Vava had three sisters—if I told you *their* names the story would never end—and the three sisters were all unmarried. One day Vava and the girls were sitting together in the second-best throne room, playing a game of Russian rummy, while outside a storm raged and ranted. In a sudden clap of thunder the ceiling of the throne-room (it was only the second-best one fortunately) burst open, letting in a good deal of rain and a very wet grey falcon. The falcon stood in the centre of the games table, shaking its bedraggled wings and looking intently at each of the three princesses. Finally it nodded decidedly and, scattering play counters wildly, changed at once into a man of distinguished appearance with silver-sided hair.

"Greetings, Prince Vladimir Nikolai Andrei Maximillian Roskatov, Czar of the Four Rivers," said the gentleman with nice formality. "May I introduce myself—the Falcon Prince at your disposal." He stepped carefully down off the games table on purpose to make an elegant bow. Vava and the princesses replied that the pleasure was theirs, and asked what brought the Falcon Prince to that part of the world.

"Briefly," said the Falcon Prince, "the wish for a wife. I would ask for the hand in marriage, Sir, of your eldest sister, who is the most beautiful girl I have ever seen." The eldest princess blushed prettily and said : "Delighted I'm sure, if my dear brother will give his permission." Vava gave it instantly, and shortly afterwards the Falcon Prince married the eldest princess and took her away to his kingdom.

In a year another such storm blew up. The ceiling of the second-best throne room had only just been repaired when a thunderbolt ripped it open again to admit a golden eagle. The bird shook a shower of raindrops all about and cast his eagle eye in the direction of the youngest princess.

In view of what had happened the previous year, no one was surprised when the eagle turned into a handsome young man with fair hair, who applied for the hand of the youngest princess with as much formality as had the Falcon Prince. And the youngest princess agreed

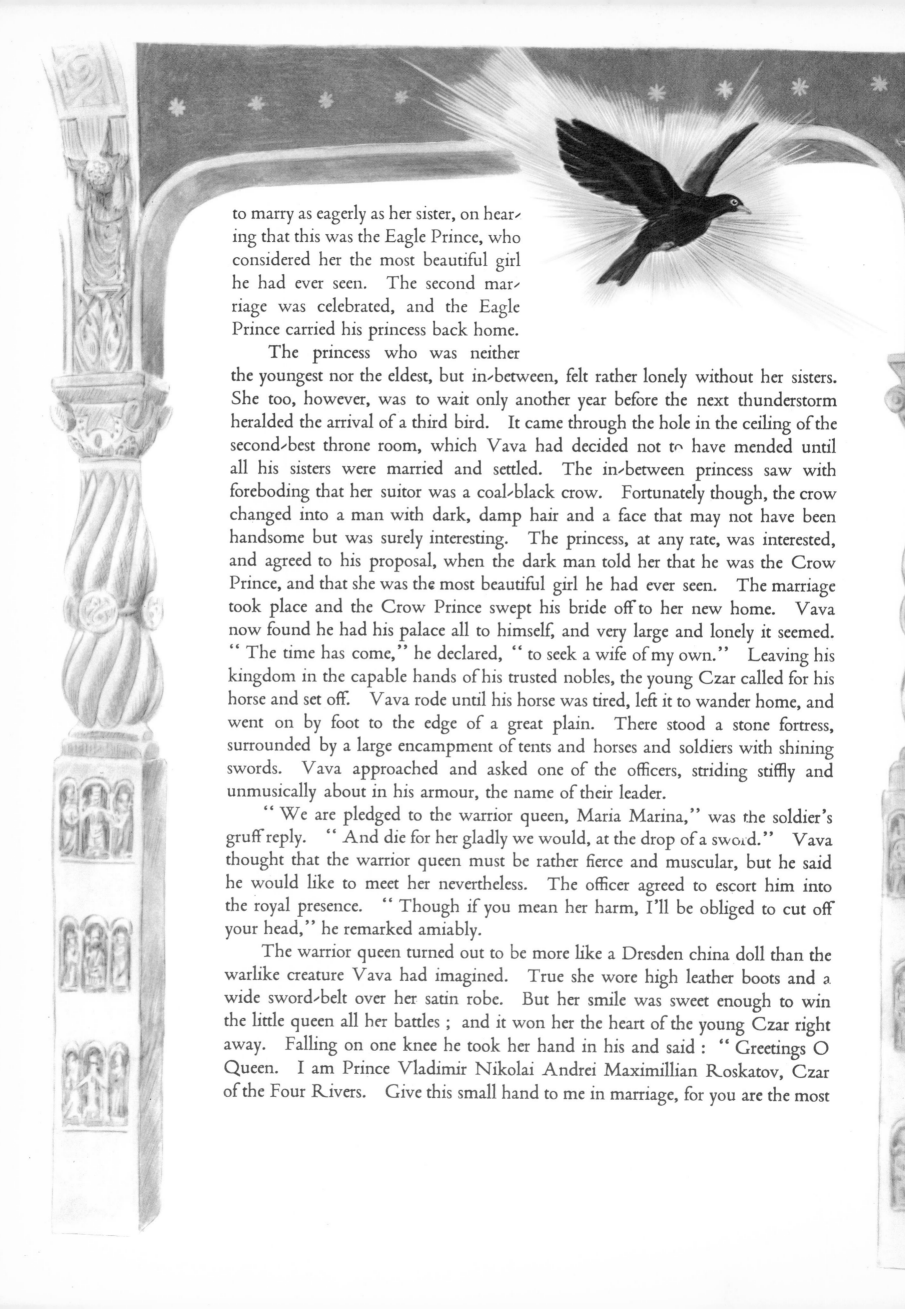

to marry as eagerly as her sister, on hear/ing that this was the Eagle Prince, who considered her the most beautiful girl he had ever seen. The second mar/riage was celebrated, and the Eagle Prince carried his princess back home.

The princess who was neither the youngest nor the eldest, but in/between, felt rather lonely without her sisters. She too, however, was to wait only another year before the next thunderstorm heralded the arrival of a third bird. It came through the hole in the ceiling of the second/best throne room, which Vava had decided not to have mended until all his sisters were married and settled. The in/between princess saw with foreboding that her suitor was a coal/black crow. Fortunately though, the crow changed into a man with dark, damp hair and a face that may not have been handsome but was surely interesting. The princess, at any rate, was interested, and agreed to his proposal, when the dark man told her that he was the Crow Prince, and that she was the most beautiful girl he had ever seen. The marriage took place and the Crow Prince swept his bride off to her new home. Vava now found he had his palace all to himself, and very large and lonely it seemed. "The time has come," he declared, "to seek a wife of my own." Leaving his kingdom in the capable hands of his trusted nobles, the young Czar called for his horse and set off. Vava rode until his horse was tired, left it to wander home, and went on by foot to the edge of a great plain. There stood a stone fortress, surrounded by a large encampment of tents and horses and soldiers with shining swords. Vava approached and asked one of the officers, striding stiffly and unmusically about in his armour, the name of their leader.

"We are pledged to the warrior queen, Maria Marina," was the soldier's gruff reply. "And die for her gladly we would, at the drop of a sword." Vava thought that the warrior queen must be rather fierce and muscular, but he said he would like to meet her nevertheless. The officer agreed to escort him into the royal presence. "Though if you mean her harm, I'll be obliged to cut off your head," he remarked amiably.

The warrior queen turned out to be more like a Dresden china doll than the warlike creature Vava had imagined. True she wore high leather boots and a wide sword/belt over her satin robe. But her smile was sweet enough to win the little queen all her battles; and it won her the heart of the young Czar right away. Falling on one knee he took her hand in his and said: "Greetings O Queen. I am Prince Vladimir Nikolai Andrei Maximillian Roskatov, Czar of the Four Rivers. Give this small hand to me in marriage, for you are the most

beautiful girl I have ever seen."

Maria Marina said that she would like to marry him very much indeed. "Though directly after the wedding I shall have to go off with my army and fight the enemy," she warned him. "Do you mind staying here to look after the fortress while I'm away? Vava said rashly that he minded nothing, so long as the queen would be his wife. So the ceremony was arranged and the wedding breakfast attended by a thousand cheering men-at-arms. It was soon time for Maria Marina to leave for the wars, and putting on her battle-dress, (silk, with a steel bodice tastefully contrived) she said : "Dear husband, here are the keys of the fortress. You may use them all except for the silver one, which opens the door at the top of the highest tower. I'd advise you not to go up there on any account." She took affectionate leave of Vava and led her army away to the wars.

Vava remained behind, as he had agreed, to look after the fortress, and felt very dull indeed after the splendour and excitement of the wedding. "I shall do whatever fighting is necessary after this," he told himself, "and Maria Marina may stay and take care of the home as a woman ought." Having done everything else there was to do, Vava's curiosity had the better of him, and he decided to try the silver key in the lock of the highest tower, despite Maria's warning. "A man's castle is his home," he reasoned,

" and there should be no secrets in it between husband and wife."   When he had turned the silver key in the lock, the door sprang open to reveal—yet another door.   Vava unlocked that door too, and indeed seven more, before he was able to enter the room beyond.   In it, bound by heavy chains, was a great ugly giant, who sat up on his bed of straw and leered cunningly at Vava.   " Come, master," he whined, " fetch a drop of water for a poor weak giant who hasn't had food nor drink for ten long years.   I've been here, alone and neglected, since the old king died, this long time past."   He rolled his eyes so pitifully that Vava felt quite sorry for him.   " You may as well have a bucket of water," he said.   " I can't see any harm in that."   Little did he guess that there was considerable harm both in the giant and in the water :   for the giant needed only a drink to regain his full strength.   Unsuspectingly Vava filled a pail at the well and brought it to the giant, who drank the whole contents in one large gulp.

With a sudden wrench the giant parted his chains as though they had been made of cotton, pushed Vava aside and went bounding out through the seven open doors and down the stairs. At this very moment Maria Marina arrived home from the wars, having successfully sent her enemies fleeing to the four corners of the earth.   She and the giant encountered each other at the gates of the fortress, and before the little queen had chance to summon her guards, she was swept off her horse.

" Put Maria Marina down ! " yelled Vava from the window, but the giant let out a piercing whistle.   Out of nowhere it seemed a fine white charger appeared, and throwing Maria Marina across the saddle, the giant climbed up behind her, and they went off like the wind.

Vava rode after them immediately, but his own horse was no match for the white charger, which soon disappeared behind the mountains.   Vava rode on and on in the same direction, but a week went by without any sign of the giant, his fast horse, or Maria Marina. On his weary journey the Czar saw a grey falcon perched on a tree.   Flying from the branch to the ground, the falcon turned into the gentleman who had married Vava's elder sister. " Why so downcast brother ? " asked the Falcon Prince, and Vava explained.

" My castle is nearby," said the Falcon Prince.   " Rest awhile with us, for you will need all your energy to foil a giant."   Vava was indeed weary, and knew that he would scarcely be a match for a midget, much less a monster, unless he stopped for a while.   His eldest sister was delighted to see him, and Vava was so coddled and fussed over that he felt like a new man when it was time to part.   " Leave us something to remember you by, dearest Vava," begged his sister, dim-eyed with regret that her brother must go.   Vava stooped and plucking a silver spur off his boot, gave it to her.   Embracing them both, Vava rode away on a fresh horse.

At the end of the second week, when Vava was again quite exhausted, he had to pass another oak tree, on a branch of which was perched a majestic eagle.   Seeing the young Czar, the eagle flew down and turned into the fair-haired man who had married Vava's youngest sister.

" Why so sad and sorry, brother ? " asked the Eagle Prince.

" My little wife, Queen Maria Marina has been captured by a giant," said Vava. "*There's* sorrow enough for any man." The Eagle Prince, seeing that Vava was about to collapse, led the steaming horse to his castle nearby, where there was a joyful reunion with the younger sister. They made him rest, eat and rest again, until Vava had entirely regained his old spirit and was ready to move onwards. Before he left, on yet another fresh horse, the youngest sister also begged for a memento, and Vava gave her the other silver spur.

It was on the fifth day of the third week that Vava, his mount staggering painfully, passed under an oak on which a black crow perched. Flying down, the crow turned into the man who had married the sister inbetween.

" Brother, your horse looks likely to drop in its tracks, and you with it," said the Crow Prince, and Vava gratefully accepted his invitation to spend the night at the Crow Prince's palace nearby.

" How delighted I am to see you, dear brother," said the inbetween princess, when they arrived. " But you look quite worn out. Come, unstrap your sword and let me pull off those heavy boots." They soon had Vava resting comfortably by the fire.

" What brings you this way ? " asked the Crow Prince, smoothing his dark hair and looking interested rather than interesting, for a change.

" I have married a queen called Maria Marina," said Vava. " Unfortunately though, a giant has stolen her away, and I am pursuing him to the other side of the mountains. The journey is certainly long and hard for one with only an ordinary horse to ride. The giant's steed must be enchanted, for in three minutes he went further than I have been able to go in three weeks ! "

After they had all had a good night's sleep the Crow Prince went out and saddled a fresh horse for Vava, who was quite ready to be off again. The inbetween princess was sad to see him go.

" Before you depart, dear brother, give me some small souvenir of your visit," she begged.

" My two silver spurs have gone to your sisters," said Vava. " But take this silver buckle from my hat. I should not like you to forget your brother, so look at it sometimes. For who knows when we might meet again ? "

Three days later Vava had crossed the mountains at last, and came in sight of a huge castle. The windows were as wide as most houses, and as for the door, its iron studs jutted out like boulders. Vava did not doubt for a moment that this was the giant's home, and that somewhere behind those strong walls, his beloved Maria Marina was shut. He tied his horse to a tree and approached by foot.

Climbing up the boulder-like studs on the door was no more difficult than rock-climbing, which Vava had done on many occasions in his boyhood. The keyhole was enormous and quite wide enough for the young Czar to creep through. Using the boulders on the other side as steps, he was soon standing on the cold flagstones within the castle. There were some stairs leading down into the gloom, and Vava guessed that the dungeon must be in that direction. Meeting nobody on the way, he followed his nose to a narrowly barred door at the end of the passage.

"Maria Marina," he called. "Are you inside?"

"Vava, I'd know your darling voice anywhere!" exclaimed Maria Marina. "You couldn't have come at a better time, for the giant is out on a two week's hunting trip. If only we could get this dungeon door open."

"The giant has locked it and left this rusty key in the lock, which is too stiff to turn," replied Vava.

"Perhaps you might find some oil in the kitchen," suggested the practical queen.

Vava went up the stairs and up some more again, until he came to the giant's kitchen, where the cutlery were the size of garden tools and the smallest pan on the stove could have held a week's washing. What it did hold in fact was enough oil to swim in. The Czar filled his hat with the oil (it was waterproof lined, against the damp) and went down to the dungeon.

As soon as the lock was thoroughly soaked with oil, the key turned smoothly, and the dungeon door swung open. Maria Marina ran out into the arms of her husband, and hand in hand they went up the stairs. Vava helped his queen to scale the inside of the front door, and through the huge keyhole they passed. On the ground below, Vava untied his waiting horse, and they rode off on its back, at a fast gallop.

When they had put a good distance between themselves and the giant's castle. Vava thought it would be safe to stop by at the castles of his three sisters, in order

that they should meet his wife. They spent a week at each different establishment. Vava and Maria Marina would not have dallied so long, however, if they had known that the giant's horse was the third fastest on earth, and that the giant rode close on their heels.

It was as they were cantering away from the castle of the Falcon Prince, towards Maria Marina's own stronghold, that the giant caught up with them. Grabbing Maria Marina in one strong arm and Vava in the other, he turned the head of his horse homewards. Struggle as they would, the unhappy pair were dragged helplessly back to the giant's castle. The giant decided to keep Maria Marina about the house for company during the long winter evenings, but he fastened Vava in a wooden keg and threw it into the sea.

Maria Marina cried dreadfully afterwards, but the giant told her rudely to be silent. "You're disturbing my afternoon nap," he complained. "That young Czar richly deserved his fate, in any case. As if he could have hoped to escape, when I have the third fastest horse on earth, to catch him with! You didn't know that now, did you, eh?"

"Where are the first and second fastest?" asked Maria Marina, with a sniff.

"Here, use my handkerchief. I can't stand snivelling women," said the giant absently. "The fastest horse and the second fastest on earth belong to the witch who lives on the other side of the Fiery River. None can cross the Fiery River but I, though, and with that very magic handkerchief you hold." Maria Marina held the handkerchief tighter, and the giant, suddenly hungry, went off to his dinner and forgot to ask for it back.

Meanwhile Vava was being tossed and turned on the waves, inside his wooden keg, and could hardly breath at all. It was only a matter of time before he would stop all together and forever. Yet, at that very moment his three sisters had all happened to take out the silver mementos that Vava had given them, for a polish and shine. To their horror and surprise the silver spurs and the silver buckle had suddenly turned a dull shade of red.

"Red is for danger!" the sisters exclaimed. "Vava is in trouble." Each princess ran to fetch her husband, and showed him the ominous sign. The Falcon prince changed at once into a bird and flew to find his brother-in-law, the Eagle Prince. The Eagle Prince had already changed into a bird too, when his wife had shown him the spur, and they both took wing to the Crow Prince. He assumed bird form as soon as he saw them coming, and together the three, flying in steady formation, went to the rescue of the young Czar. At a certain point they separated. The eagle flew over the sea, and with his eagle eye spotted the wooden keg. The falcon dragged the keg ashore with his curved beak, and the crow hastened to the Fountain of Life to fetch some water. They clawed open the keg, poured the life-giving water between Vava's dried lips, and stretched him comfortably on the shore. In a while the colour returned to the Czar's pale cheeks, his eyes opened, and he tried, though the birds would have stopped him, to sit up.

"Brothers, I owe you my life," Vava whispered. "But you must let me go, for my little queen, Maria Marina, is in the hands of the giant again."

"Let us go instead," said the eagle. "You are far too weak to attempt the journey."

"The thought of my queen makes me strong again," said Vava. "However, I am deeply grateful for your help, comrades."

"At least allow us to carry you to the giant's castle by air," suggested the crow. You will get there far sooner that way." Gripping the Czar's tunic in their beaks, the three birds swept him high above the grounds right to his destination. The crow flew into

the giant's castle, through an open window, and found Maria Marina alone in the kitchen, washing the giant's clothes. He told her that Vava was safe and intended to rescue her again.

"Let him go first to the witch of the Fiery River, and get the fastest horse on earth" said Maria Marina. "Without it, he can never outstrip the giant. Here is a handkerchief which will help him cross the Fiery River. Give it to him, and my love too, brother Crow." The crow flew back to Vava with the handkerchief and the message. Vava bade his bird-like relations a fond farewell and started on foot for the Fiery River, which was not far distant. It had been more than a day since Vava had eaten a meal, and he now grew extremely hungry. Seeing some tender young larks, he was about to draw his sword and obtain one for breakfast, when the mother lark came fluttering up. "Spare my child, I implore, lord Czar!" she cried. "One day, who knows, I may be able to help you." Vava put his sword back in the sheath and went on. Later he found a honeycomb and was about to eat it when the Queen Bee buzzed by. "Spare my honey, I implore, lord Czar," she cried. "One day, who knows, I may be able to help you." Vava continued on his way, hungry enough to eat a lion. And he found a young and tender one too, playing near its mother in a glade. But he hadn't the heart to kill the cub, for the lioness said: "Spare my child, I implore, lord Czar. One day, who knows, I may be able to help you." So Vava was obliged to contain his hunger and face the Fiery River on an empty stomach. There it was ahead of him, a crackling stream of flame, and Vava thought that trying to go across would be warm work. However, he stepped forward boldly enough, with Maria Marina's love to give him courage, and waved the giant's magic handkerchief.

Instantly a bridge of purest crystal stretched high over the Fiery River! Vava mounted it and walked to the other side, untouched by the malicious tongues of fire that darted upwards.

In front of an odd little house stood the wicked witch, trying to look as much as possible like a nice kind old lady.

"What can I do for you, young man?" she inquired, rubbing her hands together and wishing she could grind the stranger's bones instead.

"I have need for the fastest horse in the world," said Vava. "What will you take in return?"

"Your services," said the witch. "Look after my herd of horses and you shall have the fastest one in the world. But let them escape, and I shall have your head!" Vava said he thought that was fair enough, provided the witch kept to her bargain, and after a meal he was sent to take the magic horses into the meadow. Before he could shut the meadow gate, however, Vava became unusually sleepy, and sank down in a doze. For the witch had put a spell on him, hoping that the herd would escape. Then she would have an excuse to cut off Vava's head, which she was unpleasantly anxious to do.

The horses did escape, straying through the open gate and out of the meadow. It happened though, that the mother lark, whose babies Vava had spared, came down from the sky and pecked and prodded the herd back into the meadow. A sharp nip on the ear brought Vava wide awake, and he hastily shut the gate and turned to thank the lark. But the bird had flown. Vava was able to take the herd safely back to the witch, and she was furious that her plan had failed.

In the afternoon the witch sent Vava out again to the meadow, with the herd. As before Vava fell into a deep sleep, under the witch's spell, leaving the meadow gate open. The horses flocked out and would have been away but for the Queen Bee and her subjects, who swarmed among the herd, stinging them, until the horses turned tail and went back to the meadow. Then the Queen Bee stung Vava on the ear to wake him, and led her followers away, before he had recovered from the pain.

Vava was just in time, once more, to close the gate on the adventurous horses. He returned them all safely to the witch, who was more angry than ever, and determined she would have his head before the night was out. As the sun went down the witch sent Vava out to the meadow yet again with the herd. And yet again he fell asleep under her spell, without closing the meadow gate. Out trotted the horses, and would certainly have been lost but for the lionness who came strolling by. With a loud roar she sent the horses rearing upwards. Neighing in terror, they turned round and galloped back to the meadow. The lioness gave another roar in Vava's ear, which woke him at once, and after he had closed the meadow gate the lioness was no longer there. When the witch saw that Vava was putting the horses

safely back in their stables for the third time, she lost her temper, and began to turn him into a toad. Quick as a flash Vava leaped on the back of the nearest horse—it happened to be the second fastest on earth—and galloped away out of earshot, before the spell could take effect. But the old crone knew which was the fastest horse on earth, and she sprang on its back and rode after Vava. The Czar looked behind him and saw that the witch's steed was catching up on him rapidly. Reaching the banks of the Fiery River, Vava waved his magic handkerchief and the crystal bridge instantly spanned the flames. Urging his horse on, Vava was carried over the bridge, and turning saw the witch's mount halfway across. In a moment she would be upon him, with her spells and incantations, and he might never see his beloved Maria Marina again. Holding the magic handkerchief aloft, he waved it not once, but twice. At once the crystal bridge changed to spun-sugar, which cracked under the weight of the witch on her galloping horse. The hungry flames of the Fiery River licked greedily upwards and the witch and the horse fell towards them. The witch would certainly have found herself in hot water, but for the greatest presence of mind.

" Horse," she croaked, as the violent heat came to meet her, " horse, grow wings ! " At once the fastest horse on earth became the fastest horse in the heavens, for it swooped upwards, caught the falling witch neatly on its back, and flew away, not to be seen again. Now that the fastest horse was on earth no longer, but had taken to the air, no horse could beat the one Vava rode. It took no time at all to gallop back to the giant's palace, and Vava entered through the keyhole in the door, exactly as he had done on the first occasion. Maria Marina was waiting for him on the other side, the giant having gone hunting again. Up the studs of the main door they climbed, out through the tremendous keyhole, to where the now fastest horse on earth pawed impatiently. Springing on its back and hauling Maria Marina up before him, Vava sent the horse clattering away.

An enraged cry sounded in the distance. It was the giant returned on horseback from his hunting. Spurring his steed he thundered after them, screaming all kinds of dreadful threats. But soon the giant was left far behind, for Vava's horse easily out-ran his own. Grumbling angrily, the giant was obliged to turn the head of his steed and go home.

The giant's disappointment in life was great, for he had become fond, in his horrible way, of Maria Marina. And now that she was rescued and out of his grasp, the huge creature lost all interest in hunting, either for animals or humans. He stayed in the castle moping from morning until night, a mere shadow of his former self. Love had made the giant no more dangerous than any ordinary man.

And so the Czar and the Queen and the princes and the princesses all lived happily ever after, in those royal Russian times, which have never been quite the same since.

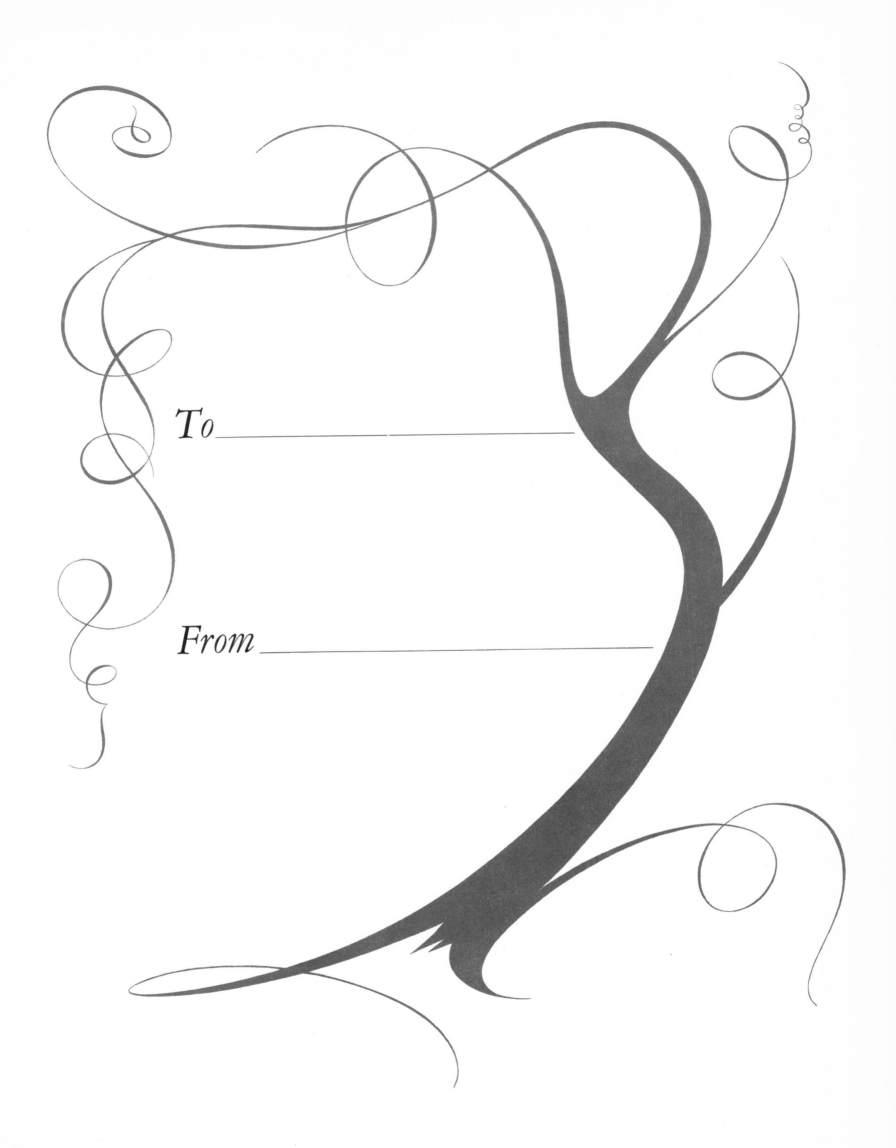

*To*_____

*From*_____

This book belongs
To _____

_____